PEDRO

PEDRO AND THE
DRAGON

by Fran Manushkin

illustrated by
Tammie Lyon

PICTURE WINDOW BOOKS
a capstone imprint

Pedro is published by Picture Window Books,
an imprint of Capstone.
1710 Roe Crest Drive
North Mankato, Minnesota 56003
www.capstonepub.com

Text © 2022 Fran Manushkin
Illustrations © 2022 Picture Window Books

Library of Congress Cataloging-in-Publication Data
Names: Manushkin, Fran, author. | Lyon, Tammie, illustrator.
Title: Pedro and the dragon / by Fran Manushkin ; illustrated by Tammy Lyon.
Description: North Mankato, Minnesota : Picture Window Books, [2022] |
Series: Pedro | Audience: Ages 5-7. | Audience: Grades K-1. | Summary:
Pedro attends a colorful parade with his friend Katie Woo and her family
to celebrate Chinese New Year, but when Katie goes missing Pedro is
ready to come to the rescue.
Identifiers: LCCN 2021004272 (print) | LCCN 2021004273 (ebook) |
ISBN 9781663909749 (hardcover) | ISBN 9781663921840 (paperback) |
ISBN 9781663909718 (pdf) | ISBN 9781663909732 (kindle edition)
Subjects: CYAC: Chinese New Year—Fiction. | Parades—Fiction. |
Friendship—Fiction. | Chinese Americans—Fiction. | Hispanic Americans—Fiction.
Classification: LCC PZ7.M3195 Pai 2022 (print) | LCC PZ7.M3195 (ebook) |
DDC [E]—dc23
LC record available at https://lccn.loc.gov/2021004272
LC ebook record available at https://lccn.loc.gov/2021004273

Designer: Tracy Davies
Artistic elements: Shutterstock: primiaou, Vector Tradition

Table of Contents

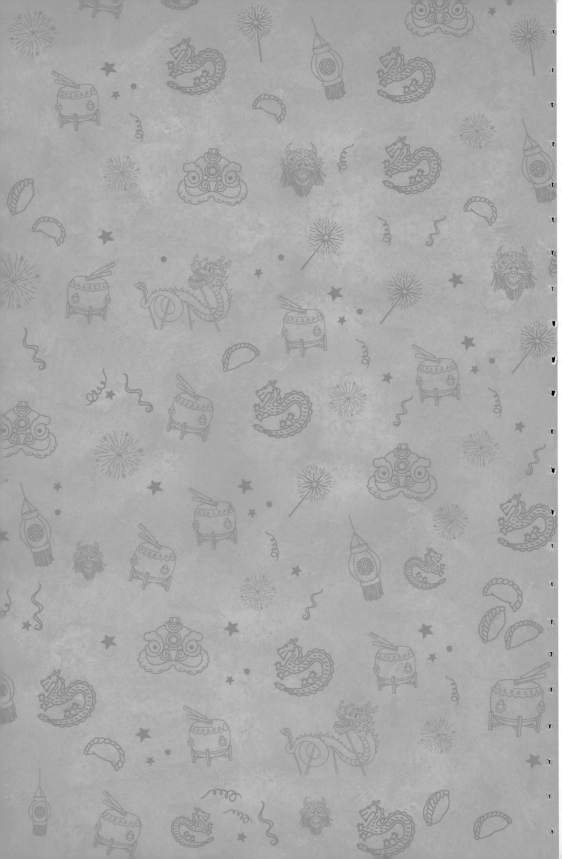

Chapter 1
Dragons and Drums

Miss Winkle told the class,

"A big holiday is coming. Soon

it will be the Chinese New

Year."

"I love it!" said Katie.

"We eat lots of dumplings."

"What else do you do on

Chinese New Year?" asked

Miss Winkle.

"We go to a parade," said

Katie. "There are big drums

and dancing dragons!"

"Can dragons dance?"

asked Pedro.

"Come to the parade and

see," said Katie.

"Cool!" yelled Pedro.

"I will."

After school, Katie told Pedro
and JoJo, "My dad and I are
making dragon masks. You can
come and make masks too."

Katie's dad showed them

pictures of fierce dragon masks.

"Wow!" said Pedro. "I want

to be fierce!"

Pedro painted his mask
blue and red and shiny gold.
He put on his mask and
roared, "I AM A FABULOUS
DRAGON!"

Katie played her drums,

and Pedro and JoJo danced.

Katie shouted, "I love the

dragons. But I love the drums

even more."

Chapter 2
Parade Time

That night, Pedro dreamed

that a dragon was chasing

Paco and Peppy.

"No way!" said Pedro.

He was brave and strong!

He scared that dragon away.

The next day was the

Chinese New Year parade.

Katie said, "I am wearing

gold shoes with red flowers.

They are the same colors as

my mask."

Pedro and his friends rushed to the parade. The crowd filled up both sides of the street.

Pedro heard the drums.

BOOM! BOOM! BOOOM!

He saw the dragons

dancing closer and closer and

CLOSER! They were awesome!

Pedro and Katie and JoJo

put on their masks. They

jumped up and down and

roared at the dragons.

Pedro danced and roared.

"I am fierce!" he yelled.

"Aren't I, Katie?"

He looked around. Katie

was gone! He couldn't see her

anywhere.

Chapter 3
Searching for Katie

Katie was small, and the crowd was big. How would they find her?

"Katie!" yelled her mom over and over. Oh, was she worried!

Katie's mom and dad and
Pedro and JoJo ran here and
there!

No Katie here!

No Katie there!

All the kids were wearing
their dragon masks. So was
Katie. How would they spot
her in the crowd?

Pedro got an idea! "Katie is wearing red and gold shoes. Let's look for them, and we will find her!"

"Great idea!" said Katie's dad.

Pedro saw green and blue and black shoes. "That's not Katie!"

He turned a corner and heard the biggest drum. "Katie loves the drum," said Pedro. "Let's follow it!"

Suddenly Pedro saw gold shoes with red flowers.

"It's Katie!" yelled Pedro.
"I found you!"

"I was chasing the big drum and got lost," said Katie.

Her mom hugged Katie over and over.

Katie's dad treated everyone

to ice cream. He told Pedro,

"You are a fierce dragon,

but a smart one too!"

"I *am*," said Pedro.

He roared all the way home.

About the Author

Fran Manushkin is the author of Katie Woo, the highly acclaimed fan-favorite early-reader series, as well as the popular Pedro series. Her other books include *Happy in Our Skin, Baby, Come Out!* and the best-selling board books *Big Girl Panties* and *Big Boy Underpants*. There is a real Katie Woo: Fran's great-niece, but she doesn't get into as much trouble as the Katie in the books. Fran lives in New York City, three blocks from Central Park, where she can often be found bird-watching and daydreaming. She writes at her dining room table, without the help of her naughty cats, Goldy and Chaim.

About the Illustrator

Tammie Lyon's love of drawing began at a young age while sitting at the kitchen table with her dad. She continued to pursue art and eventually attended the Columbus College of Art and Design, where she earned a bachelor's degree in fine art. After a brief career as a professional ballet dancer, she decided to devote herself full time to illustration. Today she lives with her husband, Lee, in Cincinnati, Ohio. Her dogs, Gus and Dudley, keep her company as she works in her studio.

Let's Write

1. Write down five facts about Chinese New Year. If you don't know five, use a nonfiction book or the internet to look some up.

2. Draw a picture of your own dragon mask. Write a sentence about what you would do if you were a dragon.

3. Have you ever been to a parade or watched one on TV? Write a paragraph to describe something you've seen at a parade.

JOKE AROUND

Which side of a dragon has the most scales?
the outside

What happens if you kiss a dragon?
You get burnt lips.

Why do dragons always sleep during the day?
They fight knights.

Knock, knock.
Who's there?
Dragon.
Dragon who?
Stop dragon your feet and get moving!

Glossary

awesome (AW-suhm)—extremely good

Chinese New Year (CHY-neez NOO YEER)—
a holiday that marks the beginning of the Chinese
Lunar Calendar; in China, Chinese New Year is
celebrated in the spring

fabulous (FAB-yuh-luhs)—very good or wonderful

fierce (FEERSS)—daring and dangerous

holiday (HOL-ih-day)—a special day or time of
celebration

parade (puh-RADE)—a line of people, bands,
cars, and floats that travels through a town or city;
parades celebrate special events and holidays

Let's Talk

1. Chinese New Year is a holiday from Katie's Chinese culture. Do you think Pedro enjoyed celebrating his friend's culture? What culture would you like to learn about?

2. Explain how Katie got lost at the New Year parade.

3. Katie's dad tells Pedro that Pedro is a smart dragon. Why do you think he said that?

What does a dragon eat for a snack?
firecrackers

What sound do you hear when dragons eat spicy salsa?
a fire alarm

Why are dragons such good musicians?
They really know their scales.

What do dragons do before a big game?
They get fired up!

HAVE MORE FUN WITH PEDRO!